KU-094-571

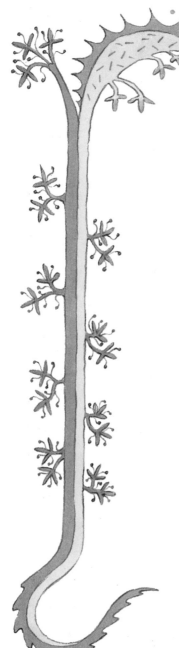

ONCE UPON A Tuesday the king was in a hurry as usual. 'Goodnight,' he said, and blew his son a royal kiss.

It missed.

Knight Tales
Three Books in One

The Kiss that Missed ⬩ Good Knight Sleep Tight
The Three Wishes

Written and illustrated by

DAVID MELLING

Hodder
Children's
Books

The young prince watched it rattle around the room,
then bounce out of the window and into the night.

The prince told the queen.

The queen told the king
and the king had a quick
word with his loyal knight.

'Follow that kiss!'
he squawked.

The knight mounted his horse . . .

. . . eventually . . .

and galloped off in hot pursuit until
they came to the wild wood.

Wild creatures with wild eyes,
too much hair and very bad manners
lived here.

It was dark.
It was smelly.
It was . . .

. . . snowing.

They were not alone.

There were bears with long claws
and growly roars, swooping owls
of all shapes and sizes . . .

. . . and a pack of hungry wolves
with dribbly mouths.

'EEK!'
squeaked the knight.
And then, suddenly . . .

. . . with a sparkle the royal kiss came floating by

and, in turn, said goodnight to everyone.

Bears stopped being growly.
Owls stopped being swoopy.
Wolves stopped being dribbly.
And before you could say 'big hairy toes'
they all settled down for a good night's sleep.

The wrinkly old
tree trunk twitched . . .

So, the knight and his
faithful horse sat down
on a wrinkly old tree
trunk to rest.

. . . and slowly rose
into the air . . .

. . . above the woods and into the clouds.

At last they found themselves staring into a pair of giant nostrils.

A dragon with 'this lot would be nice for breakfast' eyes leered greedily at them.

Suddenly . . .

. . . with a sparkle the royal kiss came floating by and flew right up the dragon's nose.

He sat up, sniffed and blinked.

Slowly, he opened his mouth,
took a deep breath and . . .

. . . sneezed!

'Hang on!' he said, as they tumbled through the trees.
'Come back!' he puffed, as he lumbered after them.

'I want to pick you up and . . .'

'. . . kiss you goodnight.'

Slowly they all made their way back to the castle.

That night the prince was happy,

the queen was happy,

and the king promised to stop
always being in a hurry.

He made sure everyone was comfortable and
slowly read them a bedtime story
from beginning to end . . .

. . . almost.

A NEW SOUND echoed along the corridors of the castle. To the king and queen was born a royal princess.

The prince had a baby sister.

He couldn't see what all the fuss was about.

Among the many
splendid presents was
the softest, fluffiest pillow
in the kingdom.

But one day
the fat royal cat
squashed it flat!

The poor princess cried.

And cried.

And cried.

So the king popped over for a little chat with his loyal knight.

'Fill this with something soft and fluffy!' he barked.

'And hurry!'

The knight leapt into action.

He was so quick there wasn't even enough time to finish the senten

Deep inside the wild wood prickly bears rubbed their grumbly tummies. 'Lunch time!' they slurped.

But the knight was thinking about his quest. 'I wonder if
I could borrow some bear hair to put in the royal pillow,'
he thought, and decided to take a closer look.

Two minutes later the grizzled bears shuffled back into the shadows, rubbing their sore bottoms and mumbling to themselves.

'Well really, it's hardly fair. We just wanted a quick nibble. No need for that ...'

Bear hair lay everywhere!

The knight filled the pillow and gave it to the horse.
'Is this pillow soft enough for the princess?' he asked.
'Neigh!' said the horse. (He thought it was too scratchy.)

Nobody noticed slinky shadows curling around the
tree trunks.

A jumble of wolves howwwled from the trees – they sniffed the knight, they sniffed the horse, then sniffed off.

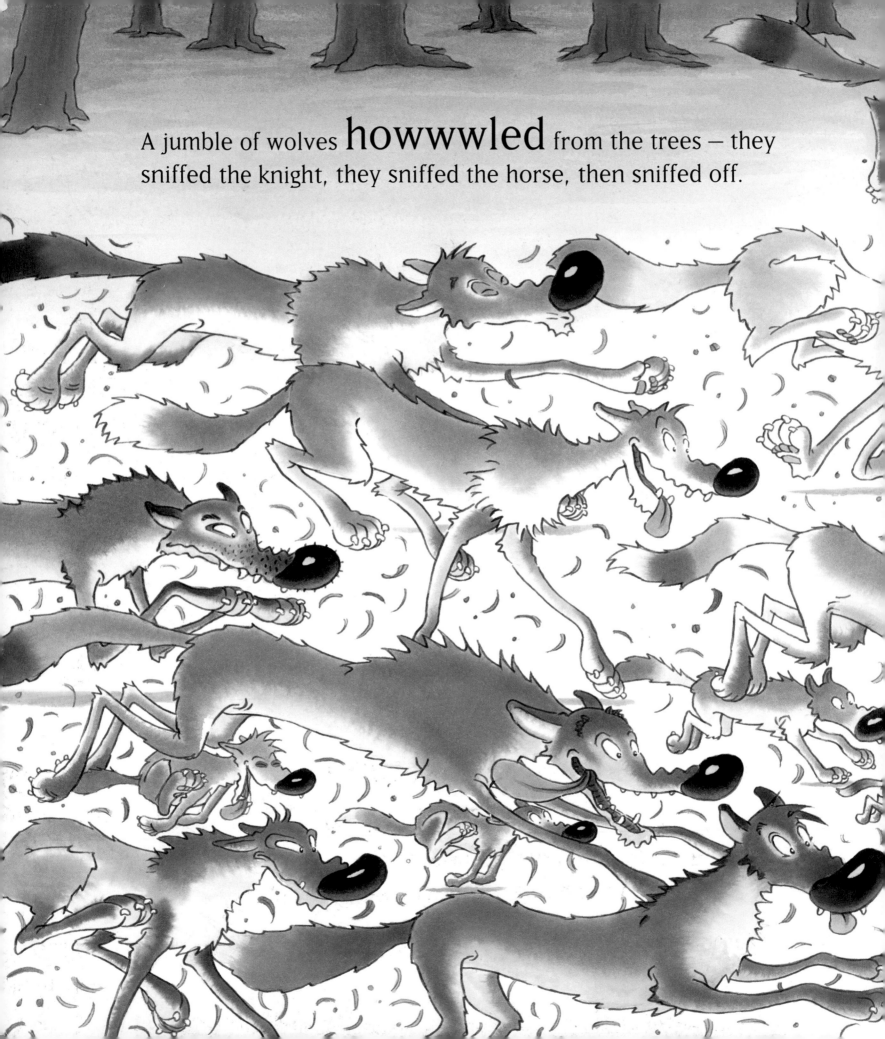

Wolf hair lay everywhere!

The knight filled the pillow again and gave it to the horse.
'Is **this** pillow soft enough for the princess?' he asked.
'Neigh!' said the horse. (He thought it was too bristly.)

Just then...

An owl

dropped out

of the sky

and bounced off the knight's head.

Feathers fluttered gently to the floor.

'That's it!' cried the knight.
'I'll make a pillow of feathers!'

'If it's feathers you want,'
said the dizzy owl, 'follow me.
I'll take you to see…

...the Feather Trees!'

So the knight and his **'I'm COMPLETELY scared of heights'** horse clambered up into the branches.

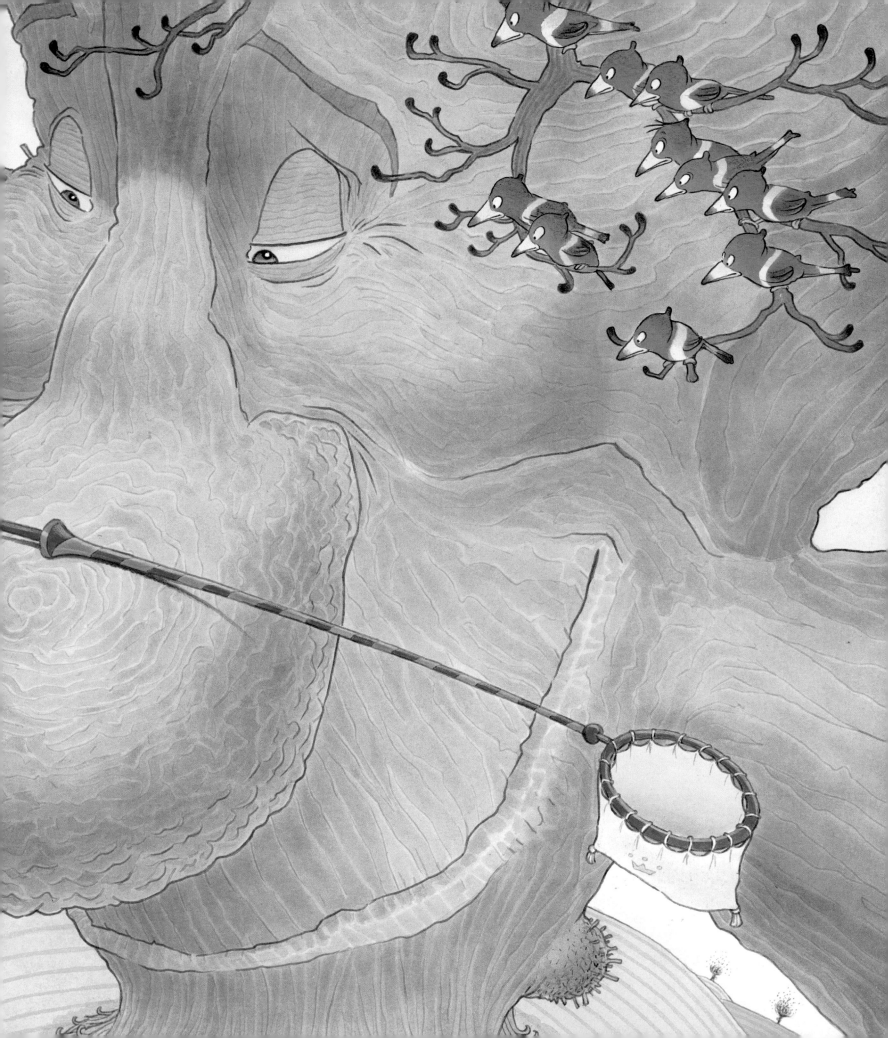

All the birds gathered round to listen
to the knight's tale. There were feathers
everywhere!

When he had finished, the birds happily agreed
to help and plucked just enough feathers to fill
the pillow to the royal brim.

The knight and his faithful horse waved goodbye
and galloped and galloped and galloped until
they came back to the wild wood.

They wrestled and wriggled their way through its
darkest secrets…

…and $plopped$ out the other side.

No one in the castle had slept for a week so they were jolly pleased to see the knight return.

'Place that child upon that pillow before I go **bananas!**'

wailed the king.

Everyone held their breath ...

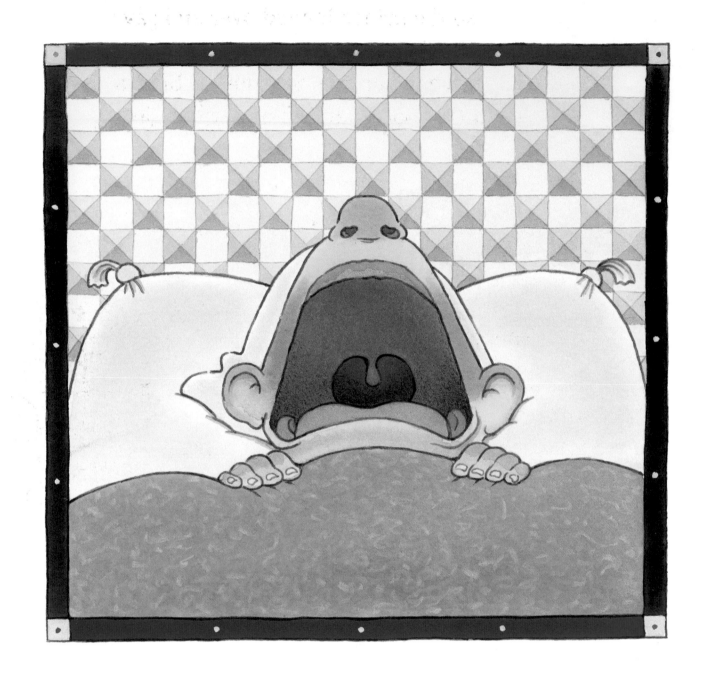

The princess didn't!

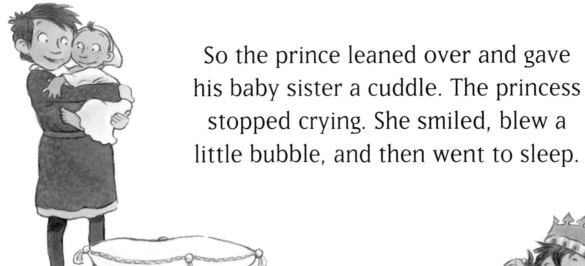

So the prince leaned over and gave his baby sister a cuddle. The princess stopped crying. She smiled, blew a little bubble, and then went to sleep.

The king hugged the prince.

The queen hugged the prince.

At last the castle fell silent …

...except for the snoring that snuffled,

sleepily through the corridors.

Good knight, sleep tight.

THE KING AND QUEEN
were away for a few days
and the knight and his
horse were appointed royal
babysitters for the weekend.
No problem, they thought.

But they soon decided that babysitting wasn't quite so easy.

And there was **SO** much to tidy up!

'I would rather fly out of this window into
a night of surprises than babysit tomorrow!'
sighed the knight.

'Neigh!' snorted the horse, which meant,
'Be careful what you wish for, because if you
believe in magic, **anything** can happen.'

Sure enough, within moments the knight and his horse
tripped and slipped and crashed through the window,
flying out into a night full of surprises.

'NOOOOOOOOOOOOOOOOOOOOOOOOOOOOOOOOooooooooooo¡

They landed in a tangled heap of arms and legs on top of a little old lady and her donkey.

'Oh dear, I've spilt my bag of spells,' she gasped. 'Hurry! If you help me catch them I shall grant you three wishes.'

The knight and his horse chased and scrambled and caught the spells one by one. It wasn't easy.

Finally, they were sure all the spells had been collected.
The old lady thanked them for their trouble and then,

with a 'poof' and a pink puff of smoke, she was gone.
But there was magic in the air.

And, oh dear, there was still one loose spell – a really, really naughty one.

The spell teased the knight, weaving its magic into his hair. The knight could only watch as the magic sprouted and grew!

'Eeek! We have three wishes!' flapped the knight.
'Quick, use one of them now.' So the faithful horse closed
his eyes and wished as hard as he could.

'**Aargh!** Our first wish is wasted!' wailed the knight. 'I don't like carrots and those fluffy slippers look ridiculous. I **wish** you hadn't done that – **oops!**'

'**Neigh! Neigh! Snort!** There goes the second wish!' whinnied the horse.

The knight and his horse were very cross with each other for wasting two whole wishes. They just wanted everything back the way it was before. Eventually, they agreed to make the third wish together.

Unfortunately, they each wished for different things —

and everything got mixed up!

'What are we going to do now?' said the knight.

'Neigh!' said the horse, which meant, 'Sit still, I have an idea.'

He took a pair of shears and set to work.

At last, they tidied themselves up, but stopped
suddenly when they heard **something** make
a funny noise.
'Oh no, now what?' groaned the knight.
'We've used up all our wishes.'

The knight panicked, so the horse panicked,
and they tried to run away.

But the naughty spell's magic was **still** growing and it snagged itself on the edge of the page. The **something** was getting closer.

It was the prince and princess.

They had come to find out who had made so much noise and woken them up!

'What's this?' they asked and pulled out the spell by its roots.

'Ouch!' said the knight.

Then the royal children led the knight and his faithful horse safely back to their room.

The next day the naughty spell had gone and the prince and princess helped tidy up the castle... inside and out. To their surprise, the knight and his horse found themselves wishing they **could** babysit the prince and princess again.

Which just goes to show,
sometimes you don't need magic

to make your wishes come true.

Well, maybe sometimes.